It's Christmas Day tomorrow!
Our house is filled with **delight**.
I'm **skipping** and **flipping**, **soaring** and *dipping*,
because ...

Santa is coming tonight!

My big sister is home, from overseas.
Auntie is here, with **frills** to her knees.
Uncle is eating crackers and cheese.

My Bum is SO CHRISTMASSY!

Dawn McMillan

Illustrated by Ross Kinnaird

SCHOLASTIC

Grandma and Pops are visiting too.
Grandma likes **singing**, and Pops likes our loo.

And of course my cousins are here!

My cousins! They are **boisterous!**

They *jump* all about.
They make **rude** noises

and they laugh and they shout ...

while I sit here, quiet as a mouse.

Mum and Dad are like **elves**, filling the shelves while Christmas smells drift through the house.

Our tree looks amazing with **bells** and a **star**.
It *twinkles* with blue and red light.
It's bright and it's **cheery** but I'm feeling dreary
because ... suddenly ... I know ...

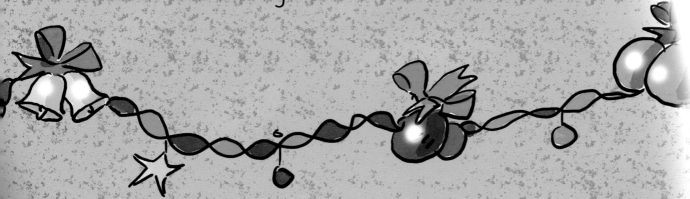

that something about me isn't right!

It's my bum can't you see – it doesn't suit me.
It's not in a *Christmassy* mood.

It's just a plain bum, in trousers red.
But I'd like a **festive** bum instead.
So ...
I'll have to wear something interesting!

Something **bold** ... like ...

Tinsel! Silver and gold.

My bum will **dazzle** and glow.

And underneath ... gold undies perhaps?

No one will ever know!

My bum will look jolly
wearing some holly,
but ... what if I have to sit?

There'll be *eeking* and **shrieking**,
squawking and **squeaking** ...

I need something softer,
something easy to wear,
like long Christmas stockings
to hang here and there.

I'd like some **sparkles**,
shining so bright.
And reindeer and snowflakes
that glow in the night.

A Christmas tree! Now that will suit me.

With layers and layers of green.

With **baubles** that glow, bows in a row

and a star where it's easily seen.

Bells will be great, to jingle all day.
Angels and snowflakes to make a display.
My bum will be stunning! A joy to
behold ...

But suddenly ...

I think about Christmas, the story we're told.

And I know ...

Yes, my thoughts are quite clear.

Christmas is special,
not a bum time of year!
It's for caring and sharing,
and not all about me.

So ...

I'll just be the boy in red trousers tonight.
I'll take a deep breath. I'll be *polite*.
I'll **smile** as I think of what my bum could be
if what I was wearing was left up to me.

Christmas morning ... Santa has been.

He's left me a gift by the tree.

It's light! It's lumpy! So **soft** and **bumpy** ...

I squeeze and I **prod**. What can it be?

I *gasp*. I **shout**. I *jump* all about!

'Perfect!' I say, my face a delight.

And then I think ...

How did Santa get my present **so right?**

About the author

Hi, I'm Dawn McMillan. I'm from Waiomu, a small coastal village on the western side of the Coromandel Peninsula in New Zealand. I live with my husband, Derek, and our cat, Lola. I write some sensible stories and lots of silly stories! I love creating quirky characters and hope you enjoy reading about them.

About the illustrator

Hi. I'm Ross. I love to draw. When I'm not drawing, or being cross with my computer, I love most things involving the sea and nature. I also work from a little studio in my garden surrounded by birds and trees. I live in Auckland, New Zealand. I hope you like reading this book as much as I enjoyed illustrating it.

Published in the UK by Scholastic, 2022
1 London Bridge, London, SE1 9BA
Scholastic Ireland, 89E Lagan Road,
Dublin Industrial Estate, Glasnevin, Dublin, D11 HP5F

Text © Dawn McMillan, 2022
Illustrations © Ross Kinnaird, 2022

The right of Dawn McMillan and Ross Kinnaird to be identified as the author and illustrator of this work has been asserted by them under the Copyright, Designs and Patents Act 1988.

ISBN 978 0702 32272 3

A CIP catalogue record for this book is available from the British Library.

Printed in Italy
Paper made from wood grown in sustainable forests and other controlled sources.

1 3 5 7 9 10 8 6 4 2

FSC
www.fsc.org
MIX
Paper from responsible sources
FSC® C023419